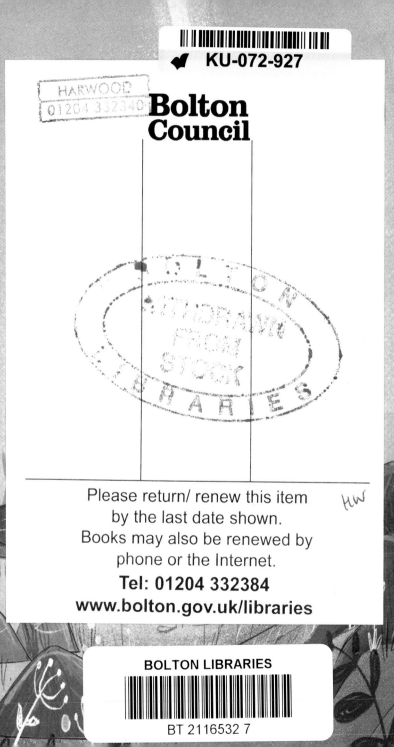

To Mia Daunt – who writes great stories
and loves Star Friends! – LC

To Lola – LF

STRIPES PUBLISHING LTD
An imprint of the Little Tiger Group
1 Coda Studios, 189 Munster Road,
London SW6 6AW

A paperback original
First published in Great Britain in 2019

Text copyright © Linda Chapman, 2019
Illustrations copyright © Lucy Fleming, 2019

ISBN: 978-1-78895-024-4

Star Friends

POISON POTION

LINDA CHAPMAN

ILLUSTRATED BY LUCY FLEMING

IN THE STAR WORLD

Deep in the glittering woods, an owl, a stag, a
badger and a wolf stood around a pool of stars
watching a picture in the sparkling surface. It
showed four ten-year-old girls, each cuddling
an animal – a fox, a squirrel, a wildcat and a
deer. The animals all had beautiful indigo eyes.

"Maia, Lottie, Ionie and Sita," said the wolf.
"They're turning out to be excellent Star
Friends."

"Indeed. They are doing a lot of good in
the human world by using magic," agreed

the owl. "Their Star Animals are helping them discover new abilities and develop their powers."

Every so often young animals from the Star World would travel to the human world. When they got there, they had to find a child who believed in magic enough to be their Star Friend. Each animal taught their Star Friend how to connect with the magical current that ran between the human world and the Star World, and then the child had to use it to help others and stop people who wanted to use magic to do evil things.

"Our young Star Animals look very happy with their friends," said the badger.

"They are but they are also facing a dangerous threat at the moment," said the owl. "The person doing dark magic near to them is very powerful, although they do not know who she is yet."

"A battle is coming," said the wolf.

The owl nodded gravely. "And it is fast approaching."

The stag looked anxious. "Let us hope our animals and their friends can win."

CHAPTER ONE

I must be dreaming. Maia shivered as she looked around. She was standing in the woods dressed only in her pyjamas. The sky had just the faintest hint of dawn light in the east.

I want to wake up, Maia thought firmly. *Wake up now!* But she didn't. Through the trees she could see the clearing where she had first met Bracken, her fox who had come from the Star World. She started walking towards it but then stopped dead. A cloaked figure was standing in the centre of the clearing, surrounded by a green circle of light. She was tearing leaves up and dropping them into a silver bowl. A chill crept down Maia's spine. She had a feeling something bad was going to happen. *Wake up,* she told herself quickly. *Just wake up!*

But she remained in the woods.

"Creeping ivy … ground elder … nightshade…" muttered the woman as she dropped the plant leaves. A large hood concealed her face. *"Come together, merge together, give me power to bind forever…"*

She waved her hand over the bowl and green smoke spiralled up. Then she pointed at a bush nearby. Small pink and white flowers suddenly bloomed all over it, buds bursting open as if it were a summer's day instead of a cold winter's night.

Picking the flowers, the woman added them to the bowl. *"And to seal the spell,"* she said. The smoke thickened and a bitter smell wafted towards Maia's nostrils.

"*Give me your power, trees!*" the woman cried.

A cold wind swept around the clearing,
blowing Maia's shoulder-length, dark blond
hair around her face and pulling at her pyjama
legs. She could feel magic crackling through
the air, prickling her skin like needles. The
trees shook and then there was a bright flash of
light inside the bowl and the clearing became
still again.

The woman laughed and, taking a silver
bottle from her pocket, she filled it with dark

liquid from the bowl. Then she straightened and held it up to the stars. "For those who would meddle in my affairs," she said grimly. "They will be sorry."

Maia felt intense foreboding sweep over her as she looked at the little silver bottle in the woman's hands.

With a laugh, the woman tucked it into a pocket of her cloak and strode from the clearing. She passed Maia without seeming to notice her, her dark cloak swishing around her ankles…

✦ ✦ ✦

Maia woke, her heart pounding. A damp nose was snuffling at her cheek. "Are you OK?" She found herself gazing into Bracken's indigo-blue eyes. "Were you having a nightmare?" he asked anxiously.

She nodded and sat up, looking around the room. She was having a sleepover with her

friends at Ionie's house. Ionie's Star Animal,
Sorrel, the wildcat, was stretched out at her feet.
Lottie was sleeping in a camp bed with Juniper,
the squirrel, snuggled against her chest while
Sita, like Maia, was sleeping on a blow-up bed
on the floor. Willow, the deer, was lying beside
Sita, her delicate legs curled underneath her, her
head resting on Sita's back. They looked very
peaceful. Maia pulled Bracken into her arms
and stroked his soft russet-red fur. His black
whiskers tickled her skin.

"Was it a magic nightmare?" he asked as he cuddled closer.

Maia pushed back her hair as she remembered it. "It was."

The Star Animals had shown Maia and her friends how to use the current of Star Magic in order to do magic themselves. The girls all had different magical abilities. Ionie could create illusions, shadow-travel and command Shades to return to the shadows where they belonged; Lottie could use magic to be incredibly agile and run super-fast; Sita could heal and soothe, and also had the ability to command people to do whatever she wanted, although she found that power frightening and almost never used it; Maia's abilities were to do with sight. She could use a shiny surface to see what was happening in other places and to see into the past and future, and her dreams often showed her things that were useful.

"What did you see?" Bracken asked.

Maia told him.

"You've had a dream like this before, haven't you?" Bracken said.

"Kind of, but not exactly the same," said Maia. Last time she had seen the cloaked figure in a dream, the figure had also been drawing energy from the surrounding trees and using it to make a potion. "There was less wind this time and no lightning and the person made a bush bloom with flowers, then used the flowers in a potion she was making. She said words that sounded like a spell." She shivered as she remembered the silver bottle the person had held up. "I don't know what she was doing but it felt like very bad magic."

"We'd better tell the others," said Bracken anxiously.

Maia glanced up at the window. Pale light was starting to streak across the night sky. "OK, let's wake them up." She went round gently shaking her friends' shoulders while Bracken woke the Star Animals. He nuzzled Juniper and Willow awake but when it came to Sorrel he gave her long tabby tail a cheeky tug.

She sprang up with a hiss and glared at him. "What are you doing, Fox?" she spat. "How dare you bite my—"

"Maia's had a dream," Bracken interrupted. "I had to wake you up quickly. Come on, pussycat."

Leaving Sorrel with her fur puffed up, he leaped back into Maia's arms. She shook her head at him but couldn't help smiling. He and Sorrel had a prickly relationship. The wildcat could be very arrogant and Bracken could be a tease.

Soon, the girls were all sitting on Maia's blow-up bed, their duvets over their legs, cuddling their animals and listening as she recounted her dream.

"So, you were in the woods and you saw someone making a potion?" said Ionie.

"Was it definitely the same person you've seen before?" asked Sita, stroking Willow's velvety, dappled-brown coat.

"Definitely," said Maia. "I couldn't see her face but I'm sure it was the same person."

"The one who's been doing dark magic in the clearing, making potions and conjuring Shades," said Willow with a shiver.

Maia nodded. The clearing was a crossing point between the human world and the Star World, and so the magic current was very strong there. A few weeks ago, the girls and animals had discovered that the clearing was withering – the spring flowers and green buds were shrivelling up. The animals suspected it was because someone was doing dark magic in the clearing, draining its power. Maia's dreams and visions had seemed to back this up.

"Do you think you were seeing something that has happened in the past or was it something that will happen in the future, Maia?" Lottie said. "Your dreams can show either, can't they?"

Maia nodded. "I don't know which it was."

"You said it was almost morning in your dream," said Ionie thoughtfully, glancing at her bedroom window. "Well, the sun's just rising now. Could you have been seeing the present?"

Maia hadn't thought about that possibility. "I

guess… I *was* wearing these pyjamas," she said slowly.

"So you could have been seeing what was actually happening as it was happening?" said Bracken, pricking his ears. "That's a clever idea, Ionie!"

"Of course it is," said Sorrel. She purred and pressed herself against Ionie's chest. "Ionie *always* has excellent ideas."

Ionie looked pleased. "If it's only just happened there may be some clues in the clearing still – clues that will help us work out who this person is," she said eagerly. "We might find a footprint or the person might have dropped something." She pushed her duvet back. "We could go and look."

"OK!" said Maia, jumping to her feet.

"But what if your mum comes in here, Ionie?" said Lottie.

"I'll leave a note saying we wanted to go for an early morning walk and I'll take my phone so she can ring me if she's worried," said Ionie. "It'll be fine."

"Um … what if we go there and the person comes back?" said Sita.

"Even better. Then we'll know who she is and you'll be able to use your magic to command her to stop!" said Ionie.

"Oh … OK," said Sita, looking a bit alarmed.

"Come on, everyone, get dressed!" Ionie insisted. Grabbing a hoody, she pulled it on over her pyjama top.

"Yes, do stop sitting around like lemons and let's have some action," said Sorrel, padding over the airbeds and stopping expectantly by the door, her fluffy tail held high in the air. "Ionie's right. There's no time to waste."

Bracken bounded over to her. "For once I agree with you, pussycat," he said, his eyes shining with excitement and his bushy tail wagging. "Let's go!"

CHAPTER TWO

Maia looked around the clearing, worry swirling in her stomach. The trees' branches were bare and even the evergreen fir trees were losing their pine needles. The grass was brown, the air smelled of damp and decay and the stream that normally tumbled and splashed down a series of rocks before flowing away into the trees was moving sluggishly.

The clearing was usually such a peaceful, beautiful place with flowers blooming and birds singing and woodland creatures scampering through the undergrowth. Now, it felt eerily quiet and still.

Bracken growled at Maia's side. "Someone has definitely been doing dark magic here."

Sorrel stalked around the clearing. "I agree. The air feels wrong – weaker."

"It smells sour," said Willow, her delicate ears flickering.

"I don't like it," said Juniper, jumping from Lottie's shoulder into her arms, his tail quivering.

"Can you smell Shades?" Ionie asked Sorrel.

Sorrel sniffed the air. "No. I think whoever has just been here doing magic has not been conjuring Shades this time."

Shades were evil spirits. They could be conjured from the shadows by people using dark magic. Once in the human world they caused trouble by encouraging feelings like jealousy, envy and fear. Only last week, the girls and their animals had found three

Shades trapped in dreamcatchers who had been manipulating people's dreams, making them behave in strange and frightening ways. They had managed to send them back to the shadows – but only just. They hadn't found out who had conjured and trapped the Shades but they were sure it was the mysterious figure Maia kept seeing making potions in the clearing.

"I didn't see any Shades in my dream," Maia put in. "I just saw a person making a potion."

"Using plant magic," Bracken added.

As well as Star Magic that the girls used, they knew there was crystal magic, which involved using the energy inside crystals, and plant magic, which involved using the properties of plants and the energy inside them to make potions.

Ionie started to hunt around. "Let's see if we can find any clues about who she is."

Maia thought back to the dream. In the

centre of the clearing the grass was flattened but there were no footprints. She looked at the bramble bush growing there and bent down to examine it. It was the bush that the woman had made burst into flower, she was sure of it. Looking at it she realized that there was another plant with long twining tendrils creeping over the top. Her eyes caught a flash of white. Carefully parting the tendrils, she saw a single white and pink flower.

She picked it.

"Look! This is one of the flowers I saw the person using," she called.

"Do you know what type of flower it is?" Sita said, coming over with Ionie.

Maia shook her head.

Ionie examined it. "I don't either. Lottie!" she called to where Lottie was rootling around in the bushes at the edge of the clearing. "Do you know what this flower is? Come over."

"Wait!" Lottie's voice was urgent. "There's something here under this bush. It's a bird. Its wing is injured."

The flower was instantly forgotten. Putting it into her pocket, Maia hurried over with the others. A mistle thrush was under the bramble bush. It was flapping one wing but the other lay useless on the ground. It started to panic as the girls crowded round.

"Oh, the poor thing," Sita said softly. "Stay back, everyone!"

They all moved away as she crouched down

and gently put her hands around the bird. Its working wing beat frantically and it pecked at her hands but she didn't flinch. "Shhh," she soothed it. "I can help you."

The fear faded from the bird's eyes and it relaxed. Maia realized Sita must be using her calming magic. Sita picked it up, gently untangling it from the brambles. The others stayed still, not wanting to scare it again.

"Its wing is broken in three places," Sita said, putting the bird on her knee and stroking its brown feathers.

"How do you know?" Ionie asked.

"I just do," Sita said simply. "It's part of my magic."

"Can you heal it?" Maia asked anxiously.

"I can try," Sita said, biting her lip. "But I've never healed a broken bone before – let alone three."

"I think it might take a lot of power to heal broken bones," said Sorrel.

"Have a go, Sita," Willow urged her. "I'm sure you can do it."

Sita took a deep breath and closed her eyes, opening herself to the current. Maia knew she would be feeling the magic sparkling and fizzing inside her. Sita placed her hand gently on the bird's wing. The others waited as the seconds passed.

After what felt like an age but was really less than half a minute, Sita opened her eyes. "I can't do it," she said, her shoulders sagging with disappointment. "I can take the pain away and I can feel the bones shifting back to where they should be but I can't make them stay in place."

"What are we going to do?" said Lottie.

"Maybe we should take it to a vet?" said Ionie.

Sita nodded. "I'm sorry," she whispered unhappily to the bird. "I really want to help you but I can't." She moved as if to stand.

"Wait," Sorrel said suddenly. "Let's think about this. Maybe if you all work together, you can help Sita."

"What do you mean?" Bracken said. "The others can't do healing magic."

"No, but they can draw on the magic current – if they all do that while touching Sita, they might be able to give her extra power."

"It could work," said Juniper, flicking his bushy tail in excitement.

"What do you think?" Maia said to Bracken.

"I think you should try," he urged. "Star Friends are supposed to work together. Sorrel's idea is a good one."

"Of course it is, Fox!" said Sorrel smugly. "I wouldn't have a bad idea, would I? Now, are you going to try, girls, or just sit around talking?"

Maia sighed. Sorrel and Ionie could be so alike – both quite annoying at times, but both extremely clever, brave and loyal.

The girls moved closer to Sita and put their hands on her. Maia felt the magic current surge inside her. It swirled around her body as it usually did, making her feel as if her blood was tingling but instead of staying inside her, she felt it flow through her hand and out into Sita. A feeling of being one with the whole world filled her.

"It's working!" Sita breathed after a few moments. "I can feel the magic power and now the bones are mending. They're fusing together. That's it!" she gasped. They all opened their eyes and saw the bird stretch both wings out and flap them. "We did it!"

The thrush opened its beak and chirruped gratefully. Sita got to her feet and gently threw it into the air. It flew off, singing as it went.

Delight rushed through Maia. "It worked!" The animals leaped around happily and the girls hugged each other.

"Thank you! Thank you for helping me!" Sita said. "It felt amazing!"

"It really did," said Lottie, her hazel eyes shining.

"It was like being swept away by magic," said Maia.

"And look – look at the clearing," said Ionie. They all followed her gaze.

The stream was flowing more quickly now and the air smelled sweeter.

"Green buds!" Lottie said, running to a nearby tree and pointing to a few small buds that had appeared on its bare branches. "And spring flowers!" she said to a patch of daffodil shoots suddenly pushing up through the soil. "What's happening?"

"Isn't it obvious?" said Sorrel.

They looked at her blankly.

Sorrel sighed. "You all know that when you use magic to do good it strengthens the magic

current," she explained. "By working together to mend the bird's wing you did some very powerful magic and that's strengthened the magic current. It's now repairing some of the damage here."

"So the more good we do, the greener the clearing will get?" said Maia.

"Exactly," said Sorrel.

"Will that work even if we're not here in the clearing when we're doing good?" said Ionie.

Sorrel nodded. "It's using your magic to do good that counts, not where you do it."

"Then we should all do lots of good deeds with our magic!" Ionie said.

"As many as possible," Bracken said.

"We can do that!" said Maia in delight.

Lottie beamed. "Good deeds, here we come!"

Willow stepped forwards shyly. "Um ... wait, everyone." They all looked at her. "Doing good will help but the only way you can properly heal the clearing is by stopping the person who is coming here to do dark magic. If you don't, she'll just keep taking the power from the trees to make her horrible potions and to conjure Shades."

There was a pause as her words sank in.

"Willow's right," Sita said heavily. "We have to find out who this person is and stop her."

"As soon as possible," Ionie agreed.

"But how do we find out who she is?" said Lottie. "Maia's tried to see her with her magic but didn't get anywhere."

"I can never see her face," said Maia. "She must be using some sort of blocking spell so she can't be identified with magic."

"So, what do we do?" said Sita.

Just then, Ionie's phone rang. "It's Mum," she said, checking the screen. She answered it. "Hi, Mum… Yes, we're fine, just out for a walk… OK. See you soon."

She ended the call. "Mum was checking we're OK. She's making pancakes for breakfast."

"Yum," said Maia, her tummy rumbling at the thought. "Maybe we'll think up a plan while we're having breakfast."

Lottie grinned. "I definitely think we should try those pancakes and see!"

CHAPTER THREE

The animals vanished as the girls left the clearing. The overgrown footpath led from the clearing, back through the trees to a stony lane. Lottie lived at the top of it, near to the main road.

As they stepped out on to the lane, Maia glanced at the thatched cottage opposite and felt her heart twinge. It had belonged to her granny before she had died the previous summer. Now, a new family lived there. A black cat was sitting on the front doorstep. It watched them with unblinking green eyes.

"Hey, Lottie!" One
of the downstairs
windows opened and
a very pretty girl with
blond hair looked out.

"Hi, Essie!" Lottie
called, going over. She
was good friends with
Essie, who had started at
their primary school a few weeks
ago. She was in Year Six, just like them, but the
others weren't so keen on her. Ionie thought
she was shallow because she only seemed
interested in talking about boys, fashion and
make-up. Maia didn't like her because she had
heard her being mean about Sita. Sita didn't
mind her – she liked everyone – but Essie made
no secret of the fact that she had no time for
Sita, who wasn't interested in fashion and often
wore her sister's hand-me-down clothes.

"What are you doing out so early?" Essie asked as Lottie went over to the little fence outside the cottage.

"Oh, we were having a sleepover at Ionie's and woke up early, so we went for a walk."

Essie's eyebrows rose. "You've been sleeping over at Ionie's?"

Lottie blushed slightly. "Yeah." She knew her two friendship groups didn't get on.

"Why shouldn't she?" Ionie challenged.

Essie acted as if she hadn't even spoken. "Well, just remember you're coming round here later with the rest of the squad, Lottie." She giggled. "And guess what, I sent a message to Taylor, Brad and Jake last night and they're coming over, too! But not until five o'clock so that will give us an hour to do our make-up and hair before they get here."

Lottie grinned. "Sounds fun! See you later."

"Yeah, later!" Essie ducked inside and shut the window.

"Sounds *fun*?" Ionie echoed as Lottie rejoined them. "Spending an hour doing your hair and make-up and then hanging round with Brad, Taylor and Jake? Seriously? What exactly is fun about *that*?"

Lottie looked defensive. "I like that kind of stuff."

Maia elbowed Ionie. The week before they had had a big fallout with Lottie over her friendship with Essie and ever since then Maia had been trying to accept that Lottie liked Essie and her "squad". "Lottie can hang round with them if she wants," she said quickly, slipping an arm through Lottie's. "Just so long as you're always best friends with us," she told her.

Lottie gave her a grateful look. "Always. You know you're my best friends and the stuff we do together will always come first, but I do like having fun with Essie and the others, too."

Ionie sighed. "I just don't get it. I really don't. You're clever, Lottie. Almost as—"

Maia trod on her foot before she could say "as clever as me" and start an argument with Lottie. Sometimes Ionie really didn't think before she spoke.

"Race you all back to Ionie's house!" Maia said hastily, setting off up the lane. "And no cheating by using you-know-what, Lottie!"

"I can beat you even without cheating!" said Lottie as she sprinted past her.

Laughing, the others charged after her, the conversation about Essie forgotten.

Breakfast was delicious – hot chocolate with fresh pancakes with a choice of syrup, lemon and sugar, jam or chocolate sauce. Ionie's mum and dad were in the kitchen, too, so the girls couldn't talk about magic but as soon as they had helped clear away, they headed up to Ionie's room.

"So, has anyone had any good ideas about

how we can find out who is doing the dark magic in the woods?" said Ionie.

"Maybe we could spy on the clearing and wait until she comes back," said Lottie.

"We could but she could go there at any time and we'll be at school in the day," said Ionie.

"One thing we haven't worked out yet is what she wants the potions for," said Sita. "What's she doing with them?"

"Perhaps the flower we found will give us a clue," said Maia. "Alice who owns the *Fairytales* shop does a little bit of plant magic. Well, why don't we go to the shop and ask her if she knows what sort of potions a flower like that might be used in?"

"That's a good idea," said Lottie.

"Though Alice doesn't know we're Star Friends," Sita reminded them. "And we mustn't tell her." The girls had learned before how important it was not to tell anyone about the Star Animals.

"No, we mustn't tell her we're Star Friends
but she already thinks we believe in magic,"
said Ionie. "We can pretend to be interested in
how plants can be used for magic and start the
conversation that way."

Maia nodded. "The shop isn't open today,"
she said, "but we could go tomorrow after
school."

"I've got gymnastics," said Lottie. "But you
three go without me. You can ask Alice about
the dreamcatchers while you're there."

The dreamcatchers the Shades had been

trapped in had come from Alice's shop. Esther, Essie's mum, had bought them from there and Essie had innocently given them out as presents. At first, the girls had suspected Alice must have put the Shades in the dreamcatchers but it had turned out she knew nothing about dark magic – she only used magic a little and she always used it for good.

Ionie nodded. "We should try to find out where they came from. Somehow the person doing dark magic must have got hold of them before Esther bought them."

"Tomorrow then," Maia declared. "We'll go to the shop and we'll find out what we can!"

CHAPTER FOUR

When Maia got home a little later, she opened the front door and found her dad in the hallway with Alfie, her little brother who was almost two.

"Come on, Alfie, get your wellies on," he was saying. "We're going to the park to meet Jack."

Alfie shook his head. "I want Thomas train." His mouth set in a stubborn line. "Not going."

"We'll find your Thomas train when we get back," Mr Greene said, looking exasperated.

"Come on, I said we'd be there in ten minutes."

"Not going!" Alfie sat down on the floor.

Mr Greene met Maia's eyes.

"Do you want me to have a look for it?" she offered.

"Thanks but I've searched everywhere. Come on, Alfie. Please."

Leaving Alfie shaking his head, Maia hurried up to her room. Shutting the door, she looked into the mirror on her desk and opened herself to the magic current.

"Alfie's Thomas train," she breathed at the glass.

The shiny surface swirled and then a picture appeared of a little blue train. Maia frowned, trying to work out where it was and then her eyes widened. It was buried in

Alfie's sock drawer!

She jumped to her feet. No wonder her dad hadn't been able to find it! She ran to Alfie's room, found the train and hurried downstairs. Alfie was struggling as Mr Greene tried to get him to stand up. "Want Thomas!" he was shrieking.

"I've got him!" Maia exclaimed, holding the train out. It was like magic. Alfie's tears dried instantly. "Thomas!" he said happily.

"Where did you find it?" Mr Greene asked Maia.

"In his sock drawer," Maia said. "I remembered I saw him putting stuff in there the other day," she fibbed.

"Phew! Thank you!" Her dad shot her a very grateful look. "Good to go now, Alfie?"

"Go park!" Alfie said, nodding cheerfully, his tantrum forgotten.

They set off. Maia shut the door behind them, feeling a warm, happy glow inside. It was lovely when she could use magic to help people. She stuck her head round the lounge door. Her fifteen-year-old sister, Clio, was sitting on the sofa reading a magazine. She was still wearing her pyjamas and dressing gown and looked like she had only just got up. Maia didn't know how she could sleep in so long. Half the day had gone! "Hi," she said, seeing Maia.

"Hi, where's Mum?"

"Upstairs, drying her hair. She's got someone coming round for coffee this morning." Clio yawned.

"Have you only just got up?" Maia asked her.

Clio nodded and looked indignant. "I wanted to stay in bed longer but Mum wouldn't let me. Hey, do you want a hot chocolate, Maia?"

"Yeah," said Maia.

Clio grinned. "Get me one at the same time."

Maia rolled her eyes. "Oh, all right."

"Love you, baby sis." Clio blew her a kiss.

Shaking her head, Maia went to the kitchen to put the kettle on. She and Clio got on pretty well most of the time. They were very different – Clio was really into clothes and make-up and shopping – but she was good at listening when Maia had friendship problems and she usually gave her good advice.

Maia made the hot chocolate, finishing each mug off with whipped cream from a can, tiny marshmallows and her favourite extra – a dollop of chocolate sauce around the rim of the mug to make it even more chocolatey. She took Clio's mug through and then went back to the kitchen. The Parents' Association at school were organizing a bring-and-buy sale on Tuesday after school to raise money to buy some new sports equipment and the children had all been asked to bake something to sell on the day. Maia liked baking and planned to make some lemon cupcakes. She started getting the ingredients out when the doorbell rang.

Maia heard her mum come downstairs and the door open. "Oh, hi, Esther. Come in," Maia heard her mum saying.

Maia pricked her ears. Esther – that was Essie's mum. The two mums came into the kitchen. Esther was carrying a small plastic bag and was looking as glamorous as ever – she had an expensive-looking poncho around her shoulders, her shoulder-length, pale blond hair was swept back in a low bun and her skin was glowing with carefully applied make-up. She and Maia's mum had grown up together in Westcombe but had lost touch after they finished school and Esther had moved away to London.

"Hello, Maia," Esther said, smiling at her.

"Hi." Maia smiled back. She had only met Esther a few times – she had her own very successful beauty product business and was often away with work – but whenever Maia met her, she was always friendly.

"Coffee?" Maia's mum asked her.

"Yes, please. Black, no sugar," Esther replied.

Maia started to weigh out her ingredients.

"Are you baking?" Esther asked her.

"Yes, I'm making cakes for the PTA sale," said Maia.

"I'm going along to that," said Esther. "I'm going to take some samples of my new anti-ageing face cream to give out in return for donations to the PTA. Speaking of which…" She took a pot out of the bag she was carrying. "I brought some round for you, Nicky," she said to Maia's mum. She smiled. "Not that I'm saying you need anti-ageing products of course!"

"Oh, I definitely do!" said Maia's mum with feeling. "I've got so many wrinkles now. If the cream helps my skin look as good as yours, Esther, I'll certainly be buying it!" She unscrewed the lid and started to rub some into her skin. "It smells delicious."

"It is very good," Esther said. "It's made from natural herbal ingredients – just like all my products."

Maia's mum spooned coffee into mugs. "I really admire you for building up your own business. How did you do it?"

"Well, after school, I didn't have the A Levels I needed to go to uni like you and Anna, so I ended up working in a health-food shop and started experimenting with making herbal beauty products. I started off selling them in the shop and soon I had people from other shops asking if they could stock them, too. The business grew from that. I still like to experiment and make products at home but now I have a team that develop the products for me once I've made the initial batch."

"Well, I'm very envious," said Maia's mum, bringing the coffee over and sitting down with her.

"Envious?" Esther frowned as she took her coffee. "Why would you envy me? You've got so much – as well as your job you've got your children, a happy family life, friends."

"But you've got those things, too," Maia's mum said in surprise. "You've got those *and* a hugely successful business."

Esther nodded slowly. "Yes. I guess."

"Hey, look what I found the other day," Maia's mum said. "This will make you smile." She rummaged among a pile of papers on the kitchen table and pulled out an old photo. "It's us when we were ten on a school trip – that one to the donkey sanctuary. Maia, come and have a look!"

Dusting her hands down, Maia went over.

"Oh my goodness," said Esther.

Maia looked over her mum's shoulder. The colours in the photo had faded slightly but she could see a group of ten-year-olds, dressed in clothes from the 1980s. "That's you, Mum, isn't it?" she said, pointing to a smiley girl with wavy brown hair, a slightly large chin and freckles.

"Yes, and that's Anna, Lottie's mum," said

Mrs Greene, pointing out the small girl next to her who had big, round glasses, a toothy smile and black hair in two neat braids. "And there's Esther."

Maia looked at a very pretty blond girl at the far end of the line of three friends, her arm around the girl next to her. The three of them were all wearing lip-gloss, had their hair in side ponytails and were wearing matching pink and lilac trainers. Maia knew instantly from their confident smiles that they were the popular girls in the class. "You look just like Essie!" she said.

"Essie really does look very like I did when I was younger, doesn't she?" said Esther with a laugh. "They say the apple doesn't fall far from the tree. School was so much fun! The best time of my life. All those friends and all the parties at secondary school."

"I didn't get invited to many parties," Mrs Greene said to Maia. "I don't remember school being quite so much fun."

Esther smiled. "It's all changed now, hasn't it? Now you seem to have a lot of friends and be very popular."

Mrs Greene smiled and clinked her coffee mug against Esther's. "To happiness and friends!" she declared.

Esther nodded. "To happiness and friends," she repeated thoughtfully.

✷ ✷ ✷

When Maia was in her pyjamas that evening she called Bracken's name and the two of them cuddled up under her duvet.

Maia giggled. "Your whiskers tickle."

He sighed happily. "I love being your Star Animal, Maia."

She kissed him. "Do you think that little bit of magic I did to help Alfie earlier will have helped the clearing?"

"I'm sure it will. Every time any of you uses magic for good – no matter how small a good deed it is – you will strengthen the magic current and that will help the clearing."

"I hope the person doesn't go back to the clearing tonight and make it worse again," Maia said. She thought about the images she'd seen. "What do you think she is making the potions for?"

Bracken frowned. "Potions made with dark magic can be used to control people or to make people feel bad feelings like jealousy, anger and greed. They'll work if they're put into food or if they're dropped on people's skin.

We must watch out for anything strange or bad happening." His indigo eyes looked serious. "I don't want anyone to get hurt."

"Me neither," said Maia. Determination flowed through her. "We won't let that happen. Whoever is making the potions better watch out – we're on their trail. We're going to find them and stop them, whoever they are!"

CHAPTER FIVE

When Maia got up to have breakfast the next morning, her mum was at the kitchen table, yawning.

"Are you OK, Mum?" Maia said.

"Do I look like I'm OK?" her mum snapped. Then she sighed. "Sorry, sweetie. I didn't mean to snap. I just really didn't feel like getting up this morning. I hope I'm not coming down with a bug." She yawned again. "I'm going to go back to bed. You're OK to walk in on your own, aren't you? Dad can drop Alfie off at playgroup for me later."

"Sure," Maia said. "I'll text Ionie and meet up with her on the way in."

"Take some money with you from my purse – you need a new school cardigan."

Just then, Clio came downstairs, pushing her tangled hair back from her face. "Why do we have to get up so early for school? I hate mornings," she moaned.

"Me, too," said Mrs Greene and, wrapping her dressing gown around her, she went back upstairs.

"I don't," said Maia cheerfully.

Clio glared at her and shoved some bread in the toaster.

"Do you like my new glasses?" Ionie said to Maia when they met up.

"Yeah," Maia said. "They look really good."

A few weeks ago, Ionie had been to the

opticians and found she needed glasses. "Do you have to wear them all the time?"

"No, just for reading from the whiteboard really but I like them."

Ionie looked over the top of them at Maia. "It makes me feel like a teacher. Maia Greene, you are in serious trouble," she said in a mock strict voice. "Stay in at breaktime."

Maia giggled. "You suit glasses."

As they arrived at school, Maia pointed to the office. "I've got to go to the office and get a school cardigan," she told Ionie. "I'll see you in the playground."

"It's OK, I'll come with you," said Ionie.

"After all, you might need protecting from Mrs Sands."

They exchanged grins. Mrs Sands, the school receptionist, who had started at the school a few weeks ago, was really bad-tempered.

She was in the school office behind the glass screen. She was about the same age as Maia's mum and was watering the array of plants she kept on the windowsill. Maia thought Mrs Sands had seen her and waited patiently but she didn't turn round, so in the end Maia tapped the glass.

Mrs Sands glanced round. "Can't you see I'm busy? You'll have to wait!" she snapped.

"Sorry," Maia apologized.

Mrs Sands finished watering the plants and came slowly over to the girls. "Yes, what is it?"

"I'd like to buy a cardigan, please," Maia said.

Mrs Sands huffed as if Maia had said she wanted to dance on the school roof. "What size?" she asked, stomping to where the boxes of uniform were kept.

"Age ten to eleven, please," said Maia.

Mrs Sands bent down with a groan and riffled through the box. "Right at the bottom, of course," she grumbled. "Here." She slapped it down on the counter and then winced and touched her back.

"Thanks." Maia paid and took the jumper. Then she and Ionie hurried outside and round to the playground.

"Mrs Sands is *so* grumpy!" Maia said.

Ionie nodded. "I wish Mrs Bramley was still secretary." Mrs Bramley had been really lovely, warm and cuddly.

They spotted Sita and Lottie and ran over to them.

"So, has anyone else done anything good with magic since yesterday?" Sita whispered as they went to a quiet place so they could talk.

Ionie nodded. "I shadow-travelled to my gran's house yesterday to fetch my mum's purse – she couldn't find it and I guessed she must have left it there in the afternoon. I told her I found it under the seat in the car."

"I helped Alfie." Maia told them about finding Alfie's train.

"And I used my magic to stop Rohan crying last night," Sita said. "He's teething and so he's been crying lots and not sleeping properly." Rohan was her baby brother.

"I did something, too. On the way home from tennis, I climbed up a tree in the park and got a kite down – it had got stuck in the branches," Lottie said.

"So, we've all done good deeds!" said Sita. "Do you think they've helped the clearing?"

"I can find out!" Maia checked no one was nearby and then pulled out a pocket mirror. "The clearing," she breathed.

An image of the clearing appeared in the glass.

"Does it look any different?" asked Lottie quickly.

Maia smiled and nodded. "The trees have got lots of green buds and the grass is growing again. There are a few more daffodils, too." She looked up. "Our magic's working!"

"Now, all we need is to find out who's doing the dark magic and stop them," said Ionie. "I wonder if we'll find anything out when we go to *Fairytales* tonight."

The bell rang and everyone in the playground started to line up. Maia and the others went over to join them – Maia and Ionie were in one Year Six class and Sita and Lottie were in the other with Essie, who was just arriving in the playground. She was with her dad. Most days she walked to school on her own but some days her dad came with her. He always looked quite odd – he had a big black bushy beard and very green eyes – and he rarely spoke.

"See you later, Dad!" Essie said. He stood there. She gave him a little push. "You can go home now." He strode off back to the school gates looking as if he couldn't wait to leave. Maia frowned. He was so different from Essie's friendly mum.

Essie ran to join her friends, Tara and Sadie, who were standing with some of the popular Year Six boys – Tyler, Jake and Brad.

"Hey, guys!" Essie twirled her ponytail and smiled round at them. "Yesterday was fun, wasn't it? You'll have to come round again."

"Your trampoline is massive," said Tyler.

"And your parents are awesome letting you order whatever you want as a takeaway," said Brad. "I'll come over any time."

"Me, too," said Tara quickly and Sadie nodded. Essie looked smug. Glancing round, she noticed Maia and the others coming over to the lines.

"Ionie!" she said. "Goodness, do you want me to do your hair?"

Ionie looked confused and touched her neat plait. "There's nothing wrong with it."

Essie raised her eyebrows. "Oh, I think there is," she smirked. Tara and Sadie giggled. Ionie opened her mouth but before she could speak, Essie cut in. "You really are going for the geek-chic look today, aren't you? Oh no, wait, it's definitely more geek than chic, isn't it?"

Ionie lifted her chin and met her cool gaze. "Actually, it's one hundred per cent geek, Essie," she said. "And one hundred per cent is exactly what I got in the maths test last week. Unlike you – didn't I hear Mr Neal saying you had to stay in at lunch and redo yours because you failed it?" She raised her own eyebrows and gave her a *so-there* look.

Tyler sniggered.

"Let's go in, guys," Essie said sharply. "Come on, Lottie. Or are you going to hang round with these nerds all day?"

Lottie glanced at Maia, Ionie and Sita.

"It's OK, go," Maia told her.

Giving them an apologetic look, Lottie followed Essie and her squad inside.

Maia usually liked school but that day she just really wanted it to be over so they could go to *Fairytales*. At the end of the day, Mrs Sands shuffled round the playground, handing out paper plates to everyone as they prepared to go home. "Here, take one of these," she said, shoving them into the children's hands. "They're for the PTA sale tomorrow." Maia looked at her plate. It had a label stuck on it with a rhyme on:

Put some cakes on me, please don't fail,
It's all to raise money at the PTA sale!

"I don't need one, thank you," said Sita, trying to hand it back to Mrs Sands. "My gran has already made a cake and it's much too big for this plate."

"Take it anyway," snapped Mrs Sands.

When Mrs Sands moved on, Sita threw it into the recycling bin in the playground.

Across the playground, Lottie was giggling as Essie pretended her plate was a hat and then turned it into a frisbee and lobbed it at Tyler.

"Lottie!" Maia called. "We're going now!"

Lottie said goodbye to Essie and ran over. "Essie's so funny," she said.

"Yeah, hilarious," said Ionie dryly.

"She is!" Lottie protested.

Maia didn't want them to argue. "Look, we'd better go. One of us will Facetime you later and tell you what happens."

"Thanks, I hope you find out something," said Lottie.

"Lottie! We'll be late for gymnastics," her mum called. "Come *on*!"

Lottie hurried off.

"Poor Lottie," said Ionie. "We're going to have far more fun." She grinned at the others. "It's shadow-travel time!" she said.

CHAPTER SIX

As soon as they got back to Ionie's house, they ran up to her room and squeezed into a patch of shadows beside Ionie's wardrobe.

"Here we go!" Ionie said, taking their hands and Maia felt the world disappear. For a moment there was grey all around her and then her feet bumped into the ground.

Maia blinked and looked around the narrow alleyway. It ran along one side of the *Fairytales* shop. There were some bins that belonged to the shop and cardboard boxes piled next to them. It was a very strange feeling to step into a patch of shadows in one place and arrive in another place a few seconds later.

The doorbell of the shop tinkled as they went inside. Maia breathed in the smell of essential oils that wafted from an oil burner behind the counter in the corner. The shop was small, but there were shelves filled with models of fairies, dragons and unicorns, as well as books on magic, herbs to help people have good dreams and creams to heal bruises. Wind chimes and dreamcatchers hung from the walls and ceiling.

Alice bustled out from the back room. She was in her sixties with ash blond hair and twinkling blue eyes. She beamed at them. "Well, hello, dearies," she greeted them. "No little pussycat with you today?"

Last time they had been in the shop they had taken Sorrel with them to see if she could smell any Shades there.

"No, my cat's at home today," said Ionie.

"Well, feel free to browse but remember, dearies, look with your eyes and not your hands," Alice said brightly. Maia only just managed to stop herself rolling her eyes. Alice always spoke to them as if they were about five.

"Actually, we came in because we wanted to ask you something," Ionie said. "We found a flower in the woods. You know lots about plants and we were wondering if you could tell us what kind of flower it is."

Maia took the flower out of her pocket and showed it to Alice.

Alice frowned. "This is bindweed. I don't understand. You can't have found it in the woods at this time of year. It only flowers in the summer."

Sita stepped closer to her. "We need you to help us without worrying and without asking any questions." Maia heard a new note in Sita's voice and knew Sita was using her commanding magic. "You must tell us what you know."

Alice nodded. "Of course I will," she said obediently. "I'll be happy to help."

"Could someone use bindweed to do something magical?" Maia asked.

Alice's mouth tightened. "Not if they wanted to use magic for good. Bindweed smothers other plants, twining around them, suffocating them. It would only be used in potions that would bring unhappiness, potions to control and harm people. If you are doing magic the herbs you want to use are good herbs like lavender and chamomile, comfrey and rosemary."

"Oh." Maia exchanged worried looks with the others. That didn't sound good. She took the flower off Alice and pocketed it. "Well, thanks."

"I've plenty of books on plant magic if you are interested," said Alice, showing them to a bookshelf. "I know you all believe in magic as much as I do and magic can be used to do a lot of good."

Maia longed to say, "We know!" She wished she could tell Alice that she and the others were Star Friends with Star Animals but last time they had told a grown-up – Auntie Mabel – it had almost ended in disaster.

Ionie started browsing the books. "These look really interesting."

Sita pointed to a metal sign above the books. "What does that mean?" she asked, her voice normal again now she had stopped using her magic.

Maia read the swirly lilac writing on the sign:
To all magic-doers, this truth be told,
Magic shall return threefold.

Alice smiled. "That's an important rule," she said. "If you do good things with magic, three times the amount of good will come back to you. If you do bad things, then you risk bringing three times the bad power back on yourself."

"It's like..." Maia broke off. She'd been about to say that it was like how doing good things with Star Magic strengthened the magical current.

"Like what?" Alice asked.

"Nothing," Maia said quickly but, catching

Ionie and Sita's eyes, she was sure they were thinking the same thing.

Alice smiled at them. "The world would be a better place if more people learned how to use magic to do good."

The girls all nodded.

"I'll come back with my mum and buy one of the books," Ionie said.

They said goodbye and left the shop. The street outside was bustling with people and they slipped into the quiet alleyway.

"So, this is bindweed," Maia said, pulling the flower out of her pocket. "And it's used in potions that can control and harm people."

Sita shivered. "You saw the figure in the woods making a potion with it. I wonder who she's planning to use it on."

"We've got to find out more about her," said Ionie. She glanced back at the shop. "We forgot to ask about the dreamcatchers. We needed to find out if someone could have put the Shades in them before they were sold in the shop."

Maia bit her lip. She'd been so busy thinking about the bindweed she had forgotten all about the dreamcatchers. "We can't go back in now."

"Wait, hang on, we might not need to. Look!" Sita pointed to the pile of cardboard boxes beside the bins. One of them – a medium-sized box – had a picture of a dreamcatcher on. "It looks like it might be the box the dreamcatchers came in."

Maia and Ionie hurried over. The box had a business name printed on it – Robinsons Home Decoration – and there was an address on it, too:

Unit 4b

Rowton Business Park

Glasgow

Scotland

Ionie snapped a picture of the address with her phone. "We could go there using shadow-travel and check it out," she said eagerly.

"We can't just appear in a warehouse," said
Sita.

"No, maybe it would be better if I used my
magic to look," said Maia.

"OK. Do it!" Ionie urged.

Maia took out her pocket mirror and said
the address on the box. The mirror swirled and
then a picture of a warehouse on an industrial
estate formed. It looked very normal. "I want
to see inside," Maia said to the mirror. The
image changed and showed her a warehouse

where people were packing different household things into boxes – mirrors, photo frames, dreamcatchers. "It really doesn't seem like the kind of place where magic is going on," Maia said, looking at the others. "It's just a warehouse. And anyway, it's miles and miles away in Scotland. The person doing dark magic lives near here – near enough to get to the woods. She can't have put the Shades into the dreamcatchers at a factory in Scotland."

"So how did the Shades get trapped in them?" said Sita.

"Maybe it was Essie," Ionie said.

"Essie!" Maia spluttered.

"Yes, after all, she gave the dreamcatchers to you, Lottie, Tara and Sadie. Maybe she's the one doing dark magic!"

"But Essie's just a normal ten-year-old!" Maia protested.

"Like us, you mean?" Ionie said, her eyebrows rising. "We do magic. Why not Essie?"

Sita shook her head. "It can't be Essie, Ionie. I know she's not very nice but she wouldn't do dark magic."

"It really isn't Essie," Maia put in. "The person I see in the woods when I use my magic is too tall. It's definitely an adult."

"Hmm. OK, maybe you're right," Ionie said reluctantly. She thought for a moment. "How about Esther then?"

Maia pictured Essie's elegant, friendly mum. "Seriously? Esther?" She simply couldn't imagine her doing dark magic.

"Why would Esther want to hurt Maia and the others?" Sita said.

"It doesn't make any sense," Maia said to Ionie.

Ionie heaved a sigh. "OK, I guess not."

They stared at each other. They'd had high hopes of going to *Fairytales* and finding out more but they didn't seem any closer to solving the mystery.

CHAPTER SEVEN

Maia's dreams contained a jumble of images that night – the school gates; Granny Anne's cottage; a silver bottle; the cloaked figure standing in the clearing, a tornado of pine needles. She also heard a laugh echoing around her. She knew it was a laugh she recognized but she couldn't work out whose laugh it was.

She woke early. "Bad dreams?" Bracken said to her, cuddling closer.

"Mmm. It's just so frustrating," Maia said. "I feel like I know the person."

Bracken licked her nose. "We'll find out who she is soon, I'm sure."

Maia thought about the potion she had seen the person making and remembered what Alice had said about bindweed being used in potions to control people. She hoped they found out soon enough – before someone got hurt.

When she eventually got up, she found her mum and Clio both sitting at the kitchen table, yawning, while Mr Greene was getting Alfie some breakfast and Alfie was drawing a picture with crayons.

Clio was examining her face in a small mirror. "I've got a spot coming on my chin," she grumbled.

"Can I use that?" Mrs Greene took the mirror off her and

examined her face. "My wrinkles are looking better. That cream of Esther's really does work. I might get some more at the school bring-and-buy sale today." She rubbed her eyes. "I just wish I didn't feel so tired."

"Can we just stay at home and have a pyjama day today?" said Clio. "I don't want to go into school."

"It's seriously tempting," agreed Mrs Greene. "I don't want to get dressed and go out."

"Mummy, look!" said Alfie, waving his picture.

"Not now, Alfie," Mrs Greene said, pushing the picture away. "I'm really not in the mood."

Maia saw Alfie's face fall. "Let me see, Alfie. It's lovely," she said as he showed her his scribbles. "Well done." She gave her mum a sideways look. It wasn't at all like her to be so grumpy in the morning. "Are you still not feeling very well?"

"I felt fine by bedtime last night," her mum said. "I'm just so tired this morning. I don't know why."

"Here. Drink this," Mr Greene said, putting a coffee down in front of her.

"Thanks," Mrs Greene sighed.

Maia got her own packed lunch ready. "I'll walk in by myself again today," she said to her mum as she got her shoes and coat on. Her mum was still in her pyjamas.

"OK, I'll see you at the sale after school," Mrs Greene said gratefully. "Bye, sweetie."

"I've got to talk to you!" Lottie hissed as they all met up at break. "Quick, let's go to the wall where it's quiet. I've had an idea."

They headed for the quietest bit of the playground. Essie was standing with Tara and Sadie and she called out to Lottie as they passed. "Hey, Lots! Where are you going? My mum bought me some new make-up in London the other day. Aren't you going to come and see it?"

"I'll see it later," Lottie called back.

Essie pursed her lips. "I might not want to show it to you later," she said.

"Oh dear, looks like poor *Lots* will miss out then," Ionie said dryly. "How will she ever cope?"

Tara and Sadie giggled. Essie swung round to them and their smiles faded instantly. "Come on, let's go somewhere else. There's a funny smell over here," she said, putting her nose in the air.

"It must be all that perfume she's wearing," Ionie commented to Maia.

Essie glared at Ionie as Maia giggled.

They walked off to the wall.

"So, what's your idea?" Sita said to Lottie.

"OK. I've been thinking and thinking about who can be doing the dark magic and I think it might be Mrs Sands the school secretary!" whispered Lottie.

They all stared at her. "Mrs Sands?" Maia echoed.

Lottie nodded. "Think about it. She started at the school about the same time as the dark magic started. She's really mean and she's mad about plants. I went into the office to take the lunch register in earlier and she was talking to them!"

For a moment they all digested the information. "She *is* about the same height as the person I've seen with my magic," Maia said slowly. "And she does have blond hair." She remembered something from her dreams the night before. "And I saw the school gates in my dreams last night. Maybe that's a clue that it's someone from school. Maybe it *is* Mrs Sands!"

"It is pretty odd that she's taken a job at a school when she obviously doesn't like children much," said Ionie thoughtfully.

"I think we should spy on her," said Lottie.

"Good plan. I'll try to watch her with my magic tonight when she's at home," said Maia, feeling excited.

Ionie frowned. "Hang on, but how did Mrs Sands put the Shades in the dreamcatchers that Esther bought?"

"I don't know," Lottie admitted. "I haven't worked that out yet."

"OK, well, for now she's our number-one suspect," said Ionie. "And we're going to be watching her like hawks!"

When Miss Harris wanted someone to collect some forms for a school trip from the office, Maia volunteered, hoping she could spy on

Mrs Sands a bit. Mrs Sands's desk was covered with paper plates filled with cakes and there were more in a big box on the floor. She was writing prices on the plates. "What do you want?" she snapped when Maia knocked.

Maia explained.

"Miss Harris should have collected them earlier. Here." Mrs Sands shoved a pile of papers into Maia's hands. "Now get out. Go on! I've got enough to do organizing the pricing of all these cakes for the sale this afternoon. All this bending and lifting is no good for my back."

Maia left, taking one last look at the array of plants growing on the windowsill. Could Lottie be right? Could Mrs Sands really be the person doing dark magic?

The bring-and-buy sale was very busy after school. Lots of parents, grandparents and child-minders turned up. Maia's mum and dad were both there with Alfie. There was a stall selling home-made greetings cards, another selling bulbs, a second-hand toy and clothes stall and one of the parents had set up a bouncy castle for the children to play on. Esther was giving out samples of her face cream, although Essie had been taken sick at lunchtime and had to go home with her dad.

"Do come and try some," Esther called out as Sita's nan passed by.

"Oh no, no, thank you, not for me," she chuckled. "I'm quite happy with my wrinkles."

"I'll have another pot," said Mrs Greene, stopping.

"It's good stuff, isn't it? Even if I say so myself," said Esther. "You should try some, David," she said to Maia's dad with a smile. She offered him an open sample pot to try from.

"Are you trying to say I look old, Esther?" he said, pretending to look offended. He rubbed some on his face. "Oh, yes, I can feel the years simply dropping away!" he chuckled.

"Sorry about him," Mrs Greene said to Esther. "I'll move him on before he drives other customers away!" Linking arms with him, she pulled him off across the playground. Maia, who had watched the exchange, saw Esther staring after them, her eyes narrowing. But then Lottie's mum walked up to the table and

Esther's face relaxed into a smile of greeting, making Maia think she must have imagined it.

"Let's go and buy some cakes," said Sita. "I'm hungry."

They went over to the cake table. Mrs Sands was supervising with some of the parents from the PTA. The cakes all looked really yummy. As they were choosing one each, Ionie squeaked. "What is it?" Lottie said, looking at her.

"I'll tell you in a minute!" Ionie whispered, her face pale.

As soon as they had paid for their cakes they hurried away from the table.

"Don't eat it!" Ionie said, swiping the chocolate cupcake out of Maia's hand just as she was about to take a bite of it.

"What? Why?" Maia said in astonishment.

"Don't you see?" Ionie said. "Mrs Sands has been in charge of the cakes all day! She could have easily slipped something into them – a few drops of a dangerous potion on the top of each cake…" They all looked at their cakes and Maia felt her appetite fade.

"You mean she could have poisoned the cakes?" she whispered, glancing over at sour-faced Mrs Sands.

"Well, probably not poisoned, but put some sort of bad magic inside them," said Ionie.

Sita stared around the playground. "But everyone's eating them! What's going to happen?"

Maia felt a chill sweep through her.

"What should we do?" said Sita.

Maia bit her lip. What she wanted to do was jump up and down and yell at everyone not to eat the cakes but she would get into so much trouble if she did that. For a start, they had no evidence – no proof that there was something wrong with them. "I guess we just watch and see what happens," she said anxiously.

Sita gulped. "I really hope everyone's going to be all right."

CHAPTER EIGHT

Maia and the others watched the playground anxiously but to their relief no one started behaving strangely.

"Maybe the cakes were OK after all," Maia said to Bracken when she got home.

"Maybe, but it does sound like this Mrs Sands might be the kind of person to do dark magic though," said Bracken. "Can you spy on her?"

Maia nodded and took her mirror from her pocket. Sitting cross-legged on her bed, she whispered Mrs Sands's name and held her breath. Would the magic show her anything? If it just showed her darkness then that might mean Mrs Sands was blocking anyone spying on her by magic and that would be a sure sign she was guilty.

However, a picture formed. It showed Mrs Sands sitting on her sofa at home watching TV. A man, who Maia guessed must be her husband, was sitting in an armchair. It all looked very normal. Maia scanned the room. There were plenty of plants in pots but absolutely nothing else unusual. *But Auntie Mabel's house looked normal*, she reminded herself. *Maybe Mrs Sands has a secret room somewhere where she does dark magic, just like Auntie Mabel had in her basement.*

As she watched, Mrs Sands rubbed her back and winced.

"How's it feeling?" her husband asked.

"Really bad today," she said.

"You must go to the doctor again," he said. "You can't go on like this."

She nodded. "I will. I'll go for a little walk later and see if that helps ease it."

It wasn't exactly an interesting conversation to listen in on. Maia spoke to the mirror. "Show me *all* the other rooms in the house," she said.

The picture changed. She saw a kitchen, a dining room, a hallway – all looked normal. A master bedroom, a spare bedroom, a bathroom. There was nothing unusual at all.

"Show me the garden," she said.

It was dusk outside but the mirror showed her a beautifully kept garden with neat flowerbeds filled with spring bulbs. A figure moved in the shadows near the lounge window. Maia caught her breath as she recognized her. Ionie! Another movement caught her eyes. She had Sorrel with her, too!

"What is it?" Bracken asked, seeing her face.

"Ionie and Sorrel are there. They must have shadow-travelled to the garden," Maia told him. She watched Ionie creep through the shadows and peep in through the window. It was such an Ionie thing to do – just to go without discussing it with the rest of them. "I hope she doesn't get caught! And anyway there's nothing for her to see there. I've had a look at the whole house." She put the mirror down and pulled out her phone. She texted Ionie.

> I know where u are! I can c u. But u can go home. I've checked it out already. It's normal. Go home! Don't get caught!!!!

She picked up the mirror again and watched as Ionie took her phone out, read her message.

Ionie grinned as she read it and then waved as if knowing Maia could see her. The next moment she and Sorrel vanished.

Maia looked up at Bracken. "They've gone home."

Just then her dad called up the stairs. "Suppertime, Maia."

"I'd better go," said Maia, putting her mirror down. "I'll come back as soon as I can."

By the time Maia had finished supper there was a text message waiting for her from Ionie.

So it's not Mrs S then?

Maia sat down on the bed and replied.

I dunno. I didn't c anything suspicious. But it still cd be I guess.

She called Bracken. He appeared and jumped on to her knee. "What now?" he said, licking her face.

"I'm not sure," she admitted.

Her phone buzzed.

Maia! I'm in the woods and the person's just gone past me and into the clearing! Sorrel won't let me stay and spy. She says it's too dangerous on my own. Can u have a look? Xx

Maia quickly told Bracken what it said and replied.

Get out of there. I'll tell u what I see. Xx

She grabbed her mirror. "Bracken! Mrs Sands said she would go for a walk later. Maybe she *is* the person doing dark magic!" She held the mirror close. "Show me the clearing!"

A picture appeared. It showed the familiar figure in the dark cloak standing in the clearing using a potion to draw a circle of green light around herself. Maia frowned. Could it be Mrs Sands? She was about the right height. Mrs Sands had blond hair and once in the past Maia had seen a strand of blond hair fall across the figure's face.

"Go as close as you can," she told the mirror.

The image of the person grew larger and larger like a camera zooming in. As she finished the circle, the trees and plants around the clearing started to tremble and shake. The figure stiffened and straightened up at once. She spun round, staring about her. "Spy!" she exclaimed wildly. Maia's heart skipped a beat. Somehow the person had realized she was being watched! "Who are you? Where are you?"

Maia gasped and cut off the magic flow. The image vanished. Maia's heart pounded as she lowered the mirror to her lap.

"What is it?" Bracken asked.

"I saw her but then she realized someone was watching her," Maia said uneasily. "I don't know how but she just knew."

"She must be using some sort of warning spell to alert her if someone is spying on her," said Bracken.

Maia didn't feel like doing any more magic after that. When she went to sleep, she hugged Bracken tightly. But in the night she had a horrible dream. She saw two eyes peering through blackness, glowing green like a cat's eyes. The spooky eyes swept from side to side and then seemed to fix on Maia. "*You!*" hissed a voice Maia was sure she knew.

Maia sat up, her heart racing in her chest. Bracken was awake instantly. "What is it?" he asked. "What did you dream about?"

She told him.

He looked worried. "We've got to tell the others about this. It sounds like the person might know who you are now!"

Maia took a shaky breath and tried to be brave. "Maybe that's a good thing. We want to find out who she is after all. Maybe if she comes after me that'll help us catch her."

Bracken nodded slowly but Maia could see the concern in his eyes.

※ ☆ ※

The girls went to Ionie's house after school. Lottie wasn't sure her mum would let her miss her piano lesson and she took the others with her to where her mum was standing with Mrs Greene to help persuade her. To her astonishment, her mum seemed OK with the idea.

"Sure, whatever," she said, waving her hand in the air. "It's no big deal if you miss one lesson. You go and hang out with your friends tonight. Nicky and I are going to The Copper Kettle for a coffee."

"Thanks, Mum," said Lottie, giving the others a surprised look.

Mrs Greene linked arms with her and gave her a nudge. "We could go to the pub after that and have a quick drink before supper."

It was Maia's turn to feel astonished. Her mum hardly ever went to the pub.

Lottie's mum giggled. "That would be a bit naughty but why not?"

"Yeah, we'll see you guys later!" Lottie's mum said.

"*You guys?*" Lottie whispered to the others as they hurried away. "Did you hear that? My mum never says *guys*."

"My mum's acting weird, too," said Maia. "I can't believe she said she wanted to go to the pub!"

She spotted her dad standing with a group of other dads near to where Alfie was playing on the climbing frame. A couple of them were miming playing air guitars. "See you at home later, Maia!" Mr Greene called. "I'm going to go and grab my guitar and have a jamming session with the boys. Get yourself some tea if Mum and I aren't home."

Maia frowned. "What's going on?" she said to the others. "My dad's not played his guitar in years." She shook her head. "I don't like this. When the adults start behaving strangely it usually means dark magic is going on."

"The cakes must have had potion in after all!" said Lottie.

"Mr Neal was a bit weird today," said Sita. "We were supposed to be having a maths test but he let us do art all afternoon and we were allowed to listen to the radio and then he pretended to drum along to some of the songs on his desk!"

"Yeah." Ionie nodded. "We were supposed to have a maths test, too, but we didn't. We just played maths games and read instead while Miss Harris kept checking her phone."

"There *must* have been something in the cakes!" said Lottie, shooting a look at where Mrs Sands could be seen sitting in the school office. "We were right!"

"But it's just adults who are being weird, not children, so surely it can't be the cakes because everyone ate them," Ionie argued. She shook her head. "This is all so confusing. I know what we should do. I think we should go to the clearing tonight – all of us together – and hide and see if the person comes. Then if she does, we try to see her face."

The others gave her dubious looks. "It's the perfect opportunity," she told them.

"Whatever's going on with the adults is stopping them worrying about us and where we are so let's make the most of it."

Lottie frowned. "But what if she sees us?"

"Sita can command her to freeze," said Ionie. "Look, Maia might be in danger if this person knows who she is. We can't just ignore that. We've got to do something and this is the best plan."

Lottie and Sita didn't look too sure but Maia nodded. She'd felt uneasy all day, as if she might be attacked at any minute. She couldn't go on like this. "Let's do it!" she said.

CHAPTER NINE

The girls dumped their bags at Ionie's house and went on down the lane to the clearing. As they passed Essie's house they heard old pop music coming from an open window. They glimpsed a figure dancing through the glass. "Looks like Esther's been affected like the other adults," said Ionie. She paused. "No, wait. That's Essie!"

Lottie frowned. "Essie wouldn't be dancing to 1980s music."

But they could clearly see Essie dancing and singing along, blond ponytail swinging.

Ionie grinned. "Who'd have thought she would turn out to have a thing for ancient pop music? Even I know that's not exactly cool."

Essie's black cat was sitting on the doorstep. It watched them with unblinking green eyes as they crossed the lane and headed down the path that led to the clearing.

As soon as they got there they called their animals' names. Bracken, Sorrel, Juniper and Willow appeared. They were delighted to see the girls. Juniper scampered up to Lottie's shoulder and rubbed his cheek against her face.

Sorrel twined round Ionie's legs while Willow butted Sita gently with her head and Bracken put his paws up on Maia's knees. She crouched down and hugged him.

"We're all together," Willow said happily.

"So much has been happening," said Sita. "We've got lots to tell you." They sat down on some tree trunks and told the animals about Maia's dream, about the strange way the adults were behaving and then Ionie told them about her plan.

"I wanted to stay last night and try to see the person's face to know if it really was Mrs Sands but Sorrel wouldn't let me."

"It was far too dangerous to be here on your own," said Sorrel. "Even for someone with your powers, Ionie." She rubbed her cheek against Ionie's arm.

Willow nodded. "Whoever we're dealing with is capable of extremely powerful magic. She could attack you and really hurt you."

"I've got an idea!" Juniper bobbed up and down on Lottie's shoulder. "Why don't you all try to use the magic current to create barriers to protect you from dark magic?"

"Like invisible shields, you mean?" said Bracken.

"Yes," said Juniper, his tufty ears twitching. "When we were in the Star World I heard that some humans can use the magical current to make defensive barriers."

"It's not a bad idea," said Sorrel, flicking her tail around her paws. "It would certainly help protect you if it works. Come on, all of you. Have a try."

"What do we do?" said Maia uncertainly.

"Connect to the magical current but instead of using it to do the things you normally do, imagine it protecting you," said Sorrel.

Maia breathed in and let the magic current flow into her. It was like turning a switch on inside her. When she connected to the magic current she felt as if sparkles were flowing through her, her body tingled and she felt somehow as if she were linked to the whole of nature. She imagined a barrier surrounding her, an invisible shield that would protect her no matter what. She saw the air shimmer and a large bubble formed around her. "I think I've done it!" she said to Bracken, who was sitting at her feet and was in the bubble, too. "I've done something, anyway. Look!"

"Well done, Maia!" said Bracken, jumping up. "I wonder if it'll protect you."

Maia glanced at the others. None of them had a bubble around them.

Sita noticed Maia's shield. "Look at Maia!" she exclaimed.

Maia tried to concentrate on staying connected to the magical current. She knew if she got distracted then the shield would disappear. "See if it works!" she told them.

Lottie chucked a pinecone at Maia. It hit the

magic bubble and bounced back.

Ionie whooped. "It does work! Go, Maia!"

Maia grinned. She was used to Sita and Ionie having all the extra powers. It felt good to be able to do something special herself.

Lottie picked up a branch and threw that but the same thing happened.

"Let me try!" said Willow. She charged at the bubble with her head down but as she hit it she bounced off and landed in a heap on the ground. She shook herself and got to her feet. "It's a really good barrier, Maia!"

"Now we just need to do it, too," said Lottie. "How did you do it, Maia?"

Maia explained and the others tried again. Lottie managed to create a weak bubble but it burst when Maia threw a pinecone at it.

Ionie and Sita couldn't make a bubble at all, no matter how hard they tried. Maia tried to help them but it was no good.

"I just can't do it," said Ionie in frustration. She glanced at the darkening sky. "We should stop trying now and hide in case the person comes along."

"Where should we hide?" said Sita, looking nervous.

"In the trees, near to the footpath but far enough back so that she won't spot us," said Maia.

The others nodded. They pushed their way into the trees, their clothes snagging on brambles. They could see the footpath to the left of them.

"Everyone stay very still and quiet," Willow whispered.

"And no rushing into the clearing when we see her," said Lottie, looking warningly at Ionie.

"No, it's too dangerous," agreed Juniper. "Just try to see her face, then we can decide what to do afterwards."

They all nodded. Sorrel stiffened. "I can hear someone coming!"

"This is it!" whispered Ionie, her eyes shining with excitement. "We're finally going to find out who she is!"

They crouched down in the shadows, hardly daring to breathe. Maia's heart was banging so loudly in her chest she was sure everyone else would be able to hear it, too. She hoped no one coughed or sneezed!

A cloaked figure came striding along the footpath. It was so strange to see the figure in real life after seeing her with magic for so long. Maia's hands grew sweaty with anticipation. They might see her face at any moment!

The person walked to the middle of the clearing and pulled out a small brown bottle. She began to use the liquid inside it to draw a green circle around herself but her hood kept her face hidden.

As the last drop joined up with the first, the trees around the clearing started to tremble. The person straightened up with a start and glared around, the large hood still hiding her face. The trees shook more violently.

"*Spies!*" the woman hissed and she swept

her arm around the clearing. A green light flashed in front of the girls, revealing their hiding place. They all blinked in the bright light, illuminated like rabbits in headlights on a road.

"You four!" The person pointed at them and almost before they knew what was happening the plants around them exploded. Brambles, thorny branches and ivy twined around them and around their animals. Tree branches swept down towards them, aiming for their faces. Sita screamed in fear, Ionie yelled and Lottie grabbed Maia and pulled her down, out of the way of a branch about to hit her head. Maia had no time to think about creating a magical barrier, she was too busy ducking and dodging the branches to be able to focus. She shouted out as a creeper wrapped around her legs, pulling her over. She thudded into the damp, leafy ground and felt the creeper tighten around her.

Bracken snarled furiously and bit through the creeper, freeing her. Juniper was gnawing frantically through brambles that had attached themselves to Lottie's wrists. Sorrel clawed at the ivy that was snaking over the girls' shoes. Lottie jumped to her feet and leaped around, using her agility and speed to grab the tree branches before they hit the others.

"We've got to get out of here!" Ionie cried.

"Go!" yowled Sorrel.

Ionie grabbed Maia and Sita's hands. "Run, Lottie! I'll bring Sita and Maia!"

"Got it!" cried Lottie.

Ionie's fingers tightened on Maia's and Maia felt the world disappear. There was a brief moment where everything was grey and then her feet hit carpet and she blinked and found herself in Ionie's bedroom. There were twigs in her hair and her face and arms were scratched and bleeding. The others looked just as bad. They all collapsed on to the carpet, panting.

"Bracken!" Maia gasped quickly. He appeared beside her, his coat matted with burrs and long brambles trailing from his bushy tail. Maia felt a rush of relief. The others called their animals, too.

"That was horrible," said Lottie shakily as Juniper leaped into her arms. "We only just escaped."

Willow and Sorrel pressed close to Sita and Ionie. Willow was trembling and even Sorrel looked ruffled.

Maia buried her face in Bracken's fur. "I couldn't create a magic barrier,' she said. "I'm sorry, there was just too much going on."

"Don't worry. I couldn't get the words out to command anyone or anything," said Sita. "It was so scary."

"She knew us!" said Ionie grimly. "Whoever it was recognized us. Did you hear what she said? *You four.* That means she knows us. I bet it *was* Mrs Sands! I wish we'd seen her face."

Maia frowned. Although she agreed that a lot of the evidence pointed to it being Mrs Sands, there was something telling her the person in the woods wasn't the school secretary. Something that didn't fit. What was it? Her voice maybe? No, it was something else.

"We didn't see her face," said Sita.

"Well, whoever it is knows who we are now and knows we're Star Friends," said Ionie.

An image of Auntie Mabel filled Maia's mind. When she had found out they were Star Friends she had very nearly managed to trap their animals and remove the memory of magic from Maia's mind. She looked around at her dishevelled friends, a feeling of foreboding shivering down her spine. This wasn't good. It wasn't good at all.

CHAPTER TEN

Sita healed everyone's cuts and scratches and
then they all went home. Maia got back to find
her parents were still being odd. Her dad was
playing on the PlayStation, her mum was doing
her nails with Clio and was letting Alfie have a
supper of crisps and biscuits.

Maia made some sandwiches for him and
for herself, then she got him into his pyjamas
and put him to bed. She didn't want to have
to try to figure anything else out that night.
Whatever was going on with her parents, they

seemed happy enough. She would deal with them another time. Right now she was more worried about herself and the others.

She wasn't looking forward to going to sleep in case those eyes appeared in her dreams again. She hugged Bracken until she dropped off.

To her relief, the eyes didn't appear, although a succession of images flashed through her mind, many the same as before: the school gates ... the silver bottle ... pine needles swirling in a storm ... trees shaking ... ivy shaking and rustling...

She became aware of Bracken licking her face. "Maia! Wake up!" he repeated urgently. She looked at him, realizing that the rustling she had heard in her dreams hadn't stopped.

She sat up. "What's happening?"

Bracken leaped off the bed and raced to her open window. "Look!"

Maia stared. A blanket of ivy was creeping over her windowsill, the tendrils crawling into her room.

She jumped to her feet and slammed the window shut. The ivy writhed as if its tendrils were snakes. She snapped the branches off and they finally stopped moving but the rest of the ivy continued to rustle as it slithered over the glass outside.

Maia backed away from the window. "What's going on?" she said in alarm.

"It's like it's spying on us," said Bracken.

Maia's phone buzzed. She grabbed it from her desk and saw Lottie had just sent a group message to her and the others.

There's ivy all over my window!

The phone buzzed again, this time with a
message from Sita.

Mine too! What's going on?

Maia typed quickly.

It's on mine too. Bracken thinks it's spying on
us.

Ionie joined in, too.

Sorrel thinks that as well. I was about to text
u. Sorrel says to try to ignore it. It'll go at
daybreak. The person's just trying to freak us
out.

Lottie's reply came straight away.

She's succeeding! U do realize this means she
must know where we all live?!!!

Maia glanced at the time. It was 4.30 a.m.
She sat down on her bed and watched the ivy
crawl over her window until the sun started to
rise. Only then did the ivy disappear, creeping
back down the wall, and finally the rustling

stopped. Maia slumped back against the pillows and rubbed her eyes with her hands. She was exhausted and she had no idea what the day was going to hold. She could feel danger closing in on them like a dark grey cloud. She wanted to stand up to it and fight it but how could she when she didn't know for sure whom they had to fight?

"I don't like this, Bracken," she said.

"I know," he agreed unhappily. "Neither do I."

★ ★ ★

When Maia went downstairs for breakfast she was relieved to find that her dad seemed back to normal. He was getting Alfie breakfast and making Maia's packed lunch.

"Where's Mum?" Maia asked.

"Refusing to get up," said her dad. He shook his head. "She stayed up until about two o'clock last night watching a film with Clio. I thought I'd better let her sleep in."

He and Alfie walked Maia to school. As they got there, Maia saw Mrs Sands getting out of her car. Maia frowned. Had the person in the clearing been Mrs Sands?

No! As she watched Mrs Sands straightening up gingerly, her hand on her back as if it was hurting, Maia suddenly realized what had been nagging at her. Mrs Sands always moved slowly, as if she was in pain, and she'd been talking to her husband about her back hurting the other night. The person in the clearing moved easily and stood straight and tall.

It's not Mrs Sands. The realization beat through Maia. Her heart plummeted. So they were still no closer to working out who it was.

Maia hurried into the playground, hoping the others would be there. She noticed that there were fewer adults than usual there. Many of those who were there were glued to their phones or yawning and looking grumpy. But some looked normal, dressed in their running gear or smart work clothes.

"Hi," Ionie said, coming over to her. She had shadows under her eyes and looked as tired as Maia felt.

"Hi," Maia said. "I need to talk to you – and the others." She dropped her voice. "It's not Mrs Sands."

"Why not?"

"I'll tell you when the others get here."

They headed over to the wall. On the way, they passed Essie standing with Tara and Sadie, and Brad, Tyler and Jake. Essie had come into school that day with make-up on – blue eyeshadow, eyeliner and red lips.

"What do you think?" she was saying,

pouting at Tara and Sadie.

"You look really cool!" said Tara.

Essie sighed. "Tara, no one says cool any more."

"Awesome?" Tara tried.

Essie sighed even louder. "It's fierce. OK? Fierce."

"Yeah, OK, Essie, you look really fierce," Tara said quickly.

"Fierce!" Ionie said, rolling her eyes at Maia.

Essie heard and turned to look at her. "You know I think it's really brave of you, Ionie," she said with a fake smile, "the way you just come to school each day not caring what you look like."

"*I'm* brave?" Ionie snorted. "I think you're brave coming to school with your face made up to look like a baboon's butt!"

The boys all burst out laughing. Essie flushed a furious bright red.

"Yeah, blushing makes you look even more like one!" said Ionie with a grin.

"I hate you!" Essie spat and she flounced away.

"Baboon's butt!" chortled Bradley.

"Nice one, Ionie," called Jake.

"You really shouldn't wind Essie up like that," said Maia as she and Ionie went over to the wall. "It just makes her mad."

"So?" said Ionie. "I don't care and neither do you. You don't like her any more than I do."

"No, I don't," Maia admitted. A grin caught at her lips. "And that *was* quite funny. Did you see her face when you said she looked like a baboon's butt?"

Ionie grinned back. "She was *FUR*-IOUS!"

They waved to Lottie and Sita, who were just coming into the playground. "Mum's still being odd," said Lottie as she and Sita joined them at the wall. "She said I can skip swimming tonight, too. Are we going to meet up?"

"Not in the woods," said Sita with a shiver. "I don't want to be anywhere near ivy or brambles right now."

Mia nodded. She felt just the same. "Let's go to the beach," she said. "We can talk there and decide what we do next. But first I need to tell you something. I don't think you-know-who is Mrs Sands."

She explained what she'd noticed in the car park.

"You're right," Ionie said. "She always shuffles around. She doesn't move like the person last night at all."

There was a rustle behind them. Maia looked round sharply. It was just some daffodils on the bank, blowing in the breeze.

After school, they headed towards the beach through the wood.

"What's that?" said Lottie, pointing to something white on the ground by the edge of the wood. She bent down and picked up a flower head. "Bindweed," she said in surprise.

"Bindweed?" echoed Sita with a gulp. "I bet the person dropped it. She might be in the clearing right now!" said Ionie.

"Let's go and see!"

"No!" Lottie gasped, grabbing her arm. "Ionie, we can't just go racing into the clearing. You know what happened yesterday!"

"But this time we'll be ready for her," said Ionie. "Sita, the second we see her you have to use your magic. Tell her to freeze."

"I really don't think this is a good idea," said Lottie.

"I agree with Lottie," said Sita.

"But this could be our chance to stop her!" said Ionie. "She's not going to be expecting us so we can surprise her. Come on!"

"No," said Lottie.

"Well, I'm going!" said Ionie, running through the trees.

"Ionie!" Maia shouted. But Ionie didn't stop. Maia ran after her. She wasn't going to let her go into the clearing alone.

As she followed Ionie, she heard a rustle. It came from the trees to the right. She glanced over and saw a cloaked figure there. "Ionie! Look!"

Ionie had seen. She leaped towards the figure, who started to hurry away. Maia charged after Ionie but as she did so, a little warning voice in her brain was telling her something was wrong. The figure didn't look quite the same as usual. It was taller and broader and was that black hair poking out from under the hood?

A laugh rang out behind them. Maia and Ionie skidded to a halt and looked over their shoulders. A hooded figure appeared behind them. Maia's blood turned to ice. *Two* hooded figures? What was going on?

"It's a trap!" Ionie exclaimed.

The figure behind them threw a handful of pine needles into the air. Almost immediately, more pine needles swirled up from the ground and swept around them, whirling faster and faster. Ionie and Maia cried out as the needles stabbed at them. They covered their faces with their arms, trying to protect their eyes. As they did so, creepers reared up and wrapped round their legs. Maia tried to kick them off but they held her fast. Her heart pounded. They were trapped! What were they going to do now?

CHAPTER ELEVEN

"Bracken!" Maia yelled at exactly the same time as Ionie called Sorrel's name. Bracken and Sorrel appeared instantly. At the same moment, the pine needles suddenly stopped whirling and fell motionless to the floor.

Bracken growled and leaped at one figure while Sorrel sprang towards the other.

"Bind them all!" the figure closest to the path cried.

Creepers wrapped round Sorrel and Bracken.

The trees near to the path started to shake.

Maia suddenly realized this was a warning to the figure – that Sita and Lottie must be coming after them. "Si—" she started to shout.

The figure snapped her fingers. A creeper *thwacked* over Maia's mouth, cutting off her warning. Looking round, she saw one cover Ionie's mouth, too, and two more wrap round Bracken and Sorrel's muzzles.

Sita and Lottie stepped through the trees with Willow and Juniper beside them. Their mouths fell open in horror as they saw Maia and Ionie and the animals imprisoned by creepers. Lottie used her magic and leaped forwards. In a second she was beside Maia and Ionie, trying to free them.

"I comm—" Sita began to say.

The figure hissed a word and a tree branch swept down. It hit Sita hard, knocking her on the head. She collapsed on the ground, unconscious. Creepers instantly twined round her, covering her mouth.

"Sita!" Maia tried to cry but all that came out was a muffled sound.

"Bind the rest, too!" ordered the figure, and before Lottie could do anything creepers snapped over her and Sita's wrists and ankles, and caught Juniper and Willow, as well.

The figure laughed. "How predictable. You each acted just as I thought you would. Did you actually think you could stop me with your feeble Star Magic?"

Maia frowned. The voice was frustratingly familiar. Who was it? And what about the other figure – the black-haired one who was now standing so silently?

"You can't bind us!" Sorrel hissed.

The Star Animals vanished to nothing in a swirl of starlight, leaving their creepers in coils on the floor. Maia was glad they had got free but she suddenly felt horribly lonely without Bracken there. Squirming wildly, she managed to prise away the creeper covering her mouth.

"Who are you?" she demanded.

"Do you really not know?" The figure laughed in amusement and shook the hood back, revealing her face, framed by blond shoulder-length hair.

"Esther!" Maia felt as if she had just had a bucket of cold water tipped over her. Beside her, she heard the others gasp, too.

"Yes, it's me." Esther smiled.

Maia looked round at the other figure – the silent black-haired one. "So, who's that?"

"I think you've met my cat?" Esther clicked her fingers and the other figure pushed its hood back, revealing Essie's dad.

"Your … your *cat*?" Maia said in confusion, wondering what Esther was talking about.

Esther smirked and clicked her fingers. In front of Maia's astonished eyes, Essie's dad changed shape, shrinking and becoming the family's black-haired, green-eyed cat. It shook itself and stalked towards Esther with a meow.

"I don't actually have a husband," said Esther. "I needed one at times, to drop Essie off at school and things like that so I used Oscar, my cat, as a stand-in. Isn't it amazing what you can do with magic?"

Maia's head whirled. So that was why Essie's dad had always seemed so odd! He wasn't human!

Lottie managed to wriggle free from the creeper covering her mouth. "Why?" she burst out. "Why are you doing all this?"

Esther smiled. "Because I can," she said.

Maia felt warm breath on her ankles and jumped. Glancing down, she saw Bracken. He had managed to sneak back and had crept through the undergrowth to her and now, hidden by the leaves, he was gnawing at the creepers tying her ankles. His indigo eyes silently met Maia's. She didn't dare say a word in case she gave him away. If he could free her then maybe she could free the others – or attack Esther in some way.

Esther was walking up and down in front of them. "Have you any idea how much money you can make with dark magic? I discovered early on that plants have the power to make people look younger. If I take the life force from a plant and make a potion with it, then add just one tiny drop into each batch of face cream, the face cream will really work. It actually can make those wrinkles melt away." She looked around the clearing. "This place – this clearing – contains astonishingly powerful magic. I realized it when I came here for a visit last autumn. I decided to move back and ever since I started using these plants and trees in my products, they have worked better than ever." She smirked.

"Of course, the latest batch of face cream has had some rather amusing side effects that I'll have to iron out before I sell it to the wider public. But it has been fun seeing the parents in Westcombe revert back into teenagers – *really* becoming younger!"

"So, that's what's been going on!" Maia realized. "Everyone who has been using the face cream has not just been looking younger but they've also been acting younger?"

"Yes, the effect only lasts as long as they use the cream but it's been amusing to watch. There will be consequences from the meetings that have been missed, the responsibilities that have not been met. Upset will follow for some time to come. Just like with the dreamcatchers I gave to you two and Tara. They brought their own problems to your families, didn't they?" She chuckled darkly. Maia felt the creeper around her ankles give way and Bracken started on her wrists.

"But why would you want to cause problems for our families?" Lottie said.

Esther's eyes narrowed. "Your mothers were geeks. They weren't supposed to be the success stories and end up with perfect lives." Her voice grew bitter. "I couldn't believe it when I came back and saw how well they had done for themselves. I wanted to upset them. I was the popular one at school. I was supposed to be happy and successful. Not them."

"But that doesn't make sense. You *are* successful," said Lottie, mystified. "You've got your business – even if it's based on dark magic – and you've got…" She looked at the cat. "Well, not a husband, but you've got Essie. What will she think if she finds out about all of this?"

Esther started to laugh. "Oh, Lottie. You think you're so smart, don't you? You're just like your mum – she always thought she was cleverer than everyone else, too. But you're not clever enough. Have you really not realized the truth?" She pulled a small gold bottle out of her pocket and held it up. "Taking the life force from the plants to make anti-ageing products may be dark magic but it's nowhere near as dark as the potion I made and put into this little bottle." She held the bottle up. "This is a real anti-ageing potion."

"What do you mean?" said Maia uneasily.

"Watch," Esther said, her blue eyes glittering. She put the bottle to her lips and drank, and in front of their horrified eyes Esther started to shiver and tremble and change – into *Essie*…

CHAPTER TWELVE

"So, what do you think?" Essie said, twirling the end of her blond ponytail. Everything about her had changed – her clothes, her hair. "You fell for it."

"You're… you're both Essie and Esther?" Maia stuttered.

"You got it!" Essie smirked. "Now, you've got to admit that's clever."

Maia glanced across at the others. Their eyes showed the horror she was feeling.

"But why would you want to pretend to be

a ten-year-old?" Lottie burst out.

"So I could re-live my youth," said Essie. "Being at school was the best time of my life and now I get to do it again but without parents telling me what to do and with all the money I need. How perfect is that? No one will be more popular than me." She shot a look at Ionie. "Although you have been trying to thwart that. Making the boys laugh at me today." Her eyes hardened. "You'll be sorry."

"You're the one who's going to be sorry!" cried Maia. "We'll tell everyone the truth."

"Like they'd believe you!" scoffed Essie. "And anyway, you won't be telling anyone anything. Not after I've used this on you." She pulled a second bottle from her pocket – it was made of silver.

Ice ran down Maia's spine. She had seen that bottle in her vision. It had the bindweed potion inside it.

"One drop of this binding potion on your skin and you'll have to do as I say. Forever." Essie smiled coldly. "I will use it on all of you and stop you revealing the truth about me."

Maia felt the creepers on her wrist loosen as Bracken silently gnawed at them. *Keep going, Bracken*, she willed him. *I've got to get free.*

She glanced across at Lottie and Ionie and saw faint movement in the undergrowth beside them. She guessed Juniper and Sorrel were trying to free them, too. Willow was the only animal who couldn't help – she was too big to creep up through the bushes and she didn't have paws or sharp teeth that were good at gnawing. Maia glanced at Sita, who was still lying knocked out on the ground, and wondered where Willow was.

"So, who should I start with?" said Essie, clearly enjoying the moment. "Ionie, I think. Just imagine all the stupid things I can make you say and do when you're bound to obey me, Ionie. Now we'll see who gets laughed at."

Ionie's green eyes flashed furiously.

Essie started towards Ionie when suddenly a blazing fire appeared in front of her.

"What..." Essie  staggered back and then her eyes narrowed as she realized it was just an illusion. "Oh, Ionie, did you seriously think that was going to stop me?"

Ionie pulled her hands up, showing that the creepers had gone, and ripped the one from her mouth. "No, I didn't think that would, but I hoped Willow might!" she cried. She nodded at the nearby trees. "Go, Willow!"

Willow came galloping out. Her usually

gentle eyes were furious as she charged at
Essie, butting her as hard as she could with
her head. Essie cried out in shock. Before she
had a chance to use her magic, Lottie was on
her feet and grabbing a creeper. She swung
through the trees, her feet connecting with
Essie's shoulders and knocking her over. Essie
sprawled on the ground just as Maia's bonds
finally broke and she leaped to her feet and
raced to Sita with Bracken beside her.

"Sita, wake up!"

Bracken started to lick Sita's face. Willow cantered to her side and nuzzled at her neck and hair. Sita's eyelids fluttered. Lottie, Juniper, Ionie and Sorrel raced over.

"No!" screamed Essie.

Maia tugged frantically at the creepers covering Sita's mouth. If Sita could speak she could use her magic.

Essie grabbed a handful of pine needles from the ground and tossed them into the air.

"Help Sita!" Maia gasped to the others as pine needles started to swirl up in a tornado again. "I'll make a magic shield."

She pictured a shield around them, protecting them. Triumph rushed through her as she saw a silvery bubble form around her friends and their animals. The pine needles battered against it, scratching and scraping, but the shield stayed strong and the needles dropped harmlessly to the ground.

Sita started to sit up. "What's happening?"

she said in confusion, peering through the silvery shield. "Why's Essie here?"

"We'll explain later," said Ionie quickly. "All you need to know is she's bad!"

Essie scrambled to her feet. "That shield won't protect you from me!" she snarled. "A shield cast by a single ten-year-old, inexperienced in using magic?" She shook her head and uncorked the silver bottle. She walked towards them. "Pathetic! One drop of this and it will dissolve instantly."

Maia's mind was working frantically. 'But it's not cast just by a single ten-year-old!" She turned to the others. "Everyone, help me, like we helped Sita before!" Maia didn't need to say any more – the others instantly understood. They all reached out and touched her.

Maia felt them draw on the magic current around them and they started channelling it into her. It flowed strongly. She felt wonderfully powerful as she focused on the shield. Suddenly it started to glow. Rainbow colours streamed across its surface, and light sparked off it just as Essie threw the contents of the bottle.

The potion hit the surface and rebounded, splashing all over Essie. She screamed and collapsed on the ground, changing back into Esther as she did so. Sita gasped in shock. "She's Esther!" The others nodded as the plants instantly released their grip on the girls.

"What have you done?" Esther panted hoarsely, glaring at them from the ground. "I can't move!"

"What's happening?" Maia said to Bracken.

"I don't know," he said.

"I believe I do! It's the threefold rule of magic," said Sorrel. "The evil she intended when she threw the potion has returned to her three times as strongly. The binding spell has tripled in power." She looked smugly at Esther. "Now she can't do anything without your command."

"No!" screamed Esther.

The girls looked at each other. Maia broke the connection with the current and the bubble evaporated into a shower of glittery sparkles. "What do we do?" she said to the others.

"I don't want her under our command," said Lottie.

"Leave this to me," said Ionie. She walked over to Esther. "We command you to leave Westcombe," she said firmly. "You must never be Essie again. You must stay as Esther and you must only use your magic for good from now on. If you do anything else, you will … you will … explode!" she finished.

"Explode?" Maia exclaimed, glancing at Esther, who looked horrified.

Ionie grinned. "I couldn't think of anything else."

"I'm really glad Sita's the one who usually does the commanding," said Lottie. Sita gave her a weak smile. "But yes, I guess you're right in this case. You must be good from now on and get older like normal people do," she told Esther.

"Now get up and go home without saying anything," said Ionie. "Oh, and I also command you to give your cat some treats. It's not his fault that you used magic on him."

Glaring at her, Esther got to her feet. With a toss of her hair, she turned and stalked off into the trees, the cat following at her heels.

"We did it," said Ionie, looking at the others as the animals jumped around them – barking, meowing, bleating and chattering.

"Will someone please tell me what's going on?" said Sita in confusion.

They quickly explained.

"So, Esther was Essie and Essie was Esther all along?" Sita shook her head in astonishment. "Esther was doing the dark magic?" She rubbed her head. "Ouch. I've got a massive lump. I wish I could heal myself but healing magic only works on other people."

Willow inspected the bump. "It should get better soon."

"And I guess it's definitely worth having a lump if it means we've stopped the dark magic," said Sita, stroking her.

"I told you we were right to come into the clearing and see what was going on," Ionie said to Lottie.

"Right?" spluttered Lottie. "We almost got killed, or at least bound to do her bidding forever!"

"It was very scary!" said Juniper, taking a flying leap on to Lottie's head.

"It wasn't that bad,' said Ionie airily. She nudged Maia. "Thanks for coming after me."

"No probs, but next time, maybe let's think about it – at least for a few seconds first," said Maia.

"Maybe," said Ionie, with a grin. "Maybe not."

"Look, everyone!" said Sita. "Look what's happening!"

All around them, the clearing was healing itself. The withered trees straightened up, green leaves sprouting on their branches and pine needles reappearing on the branches. Bright daffodils pushed up through the ground and the waterfall started to flow with sparkling water that rushed away, over the stones and down to the sea in a glittering stream. Birds swooped through the branches.

"It looks beautiful!" said Willow.

"It's the threefold rule again," said Sorrel, walking around the clearing. "The good you've just done has come back threefold. The magic has been strengthened so much the clearing is rejuvenating and returning to normal."

Bracken barked in excitement. Willow bucked and Juniper raced up the tree trunks and leaped from branch to branch.

"We did it! We did it!" said Maia, grabbing Ionie's hands and swinging her round. She imagined her granny smiling down at her from wherever she was and knew she would be feeling very proud. "We saved the clearing!"

"And we did some awesome magic together!" said Ionie happily.

"There's always something new to learn about magic," said Lottie. "That's why I love it so much."

"Me, too." Maia smiled. "I can't wait to learn even more!" She held out her arms and Bracken jumped into them.

"Whatever comes along next we'll be ready for it," he said, licking her nose.

"Ready and waiting," Maia agreed, hugging him tightly.

A week later, the girls stood on the lane by the footpath watching the last of Esther's possessions being loaded into a removal lorry. None of them had seen Esther since the evening in the woods. According to Maia's mum, she'd decided she couldn't live so far away from London and so the family had moved back.

The totally made-up, pretend family, Maia thought.

"I wonder what will happen to your granny's house now," Sita said to Maia. "Hopefully someone nice will move in."

"Esther seemed nice," said Maia. She shook her head. "It's so hard to tell with people, isn't it? You meet someone and think one thing about them and they turn out to be totally different."

"Like Mrs Sands," said Ionie. "She's been much friendlier this week."

"I went into the office when she was there and used my magic to heal her back," said Sita. "My nan says Mrs Sands thinks she's feeling better because she got some new painkillers from the doctor. I don't mind what she thinks, I'm just glad she's happier now. It was the pain that was making her so grumpy."

"I feel bad we suspected her," said Lottie. "It's difficult to know who to trust though."

Maia linked arms with her. "We can trust each other. At least we know that."

"And Sorrel, Bracken, Willow and Juniper," added Ionie.

"Let's go to the clearing and see them," said Sita eagerly. "We can try combining our magic again."

"And I want to have another go at making a magic barrier," said Lottie. "I'm sure I'll be able to do it one day if I keep practising."

"Race you all there!" Maia said.

She set off down the woodland path, pushing through the undergrowth and bursting out into the clearing. It looked very different to how it did a few weeks ago. The waterfall was rushing merrily over the rocks, the water glinting in the sunlight. The trees' branches were covered with new leaves, bluebells carpeted the forest floor among the tree trunks and swathes of pretty pink flowers edged the soft grass of the clearing. The air smelled fresh and sweet.

The girls called their animals' names. Bracken, Willow, Juniper and Sorrel appeared and gambolled around the girls.

Happiness rushed through Maia as Bracken bounded into her arms, his beautiful indigo eyes shining. "Is it magic time, Maia?" he asked eagerly.

Maia grinned and kissed him on the nose. "Oh, yes!" she said. "It always is!"

About the Author

Linda Chapman is the best–selling author of over 200 books. The biggest compliment Linda can have is for a child to tell her they became a reader after reading one of her books. Linda lives in a cottage with a tower in Leicestershire with her husband, three children, three dogs and three ponies. When she's not writing, Linda likes to ride, read and visit schools and libraries to talk to people about writing.

www.lindachapmanauthor.co.uk

About the Illustrator

Lucy Fleming has been an avid doodler and bookworm since early childhood. Drawing always seemed like so much fun but she never dreamed it could be a full-time job! She lives and works in a small town in England with her partner and a little black cat. When not at her desk she likes nothing more than to be outdoors in the sunshine with a hot cup of tea.

www.lucyflemingillustrations.com